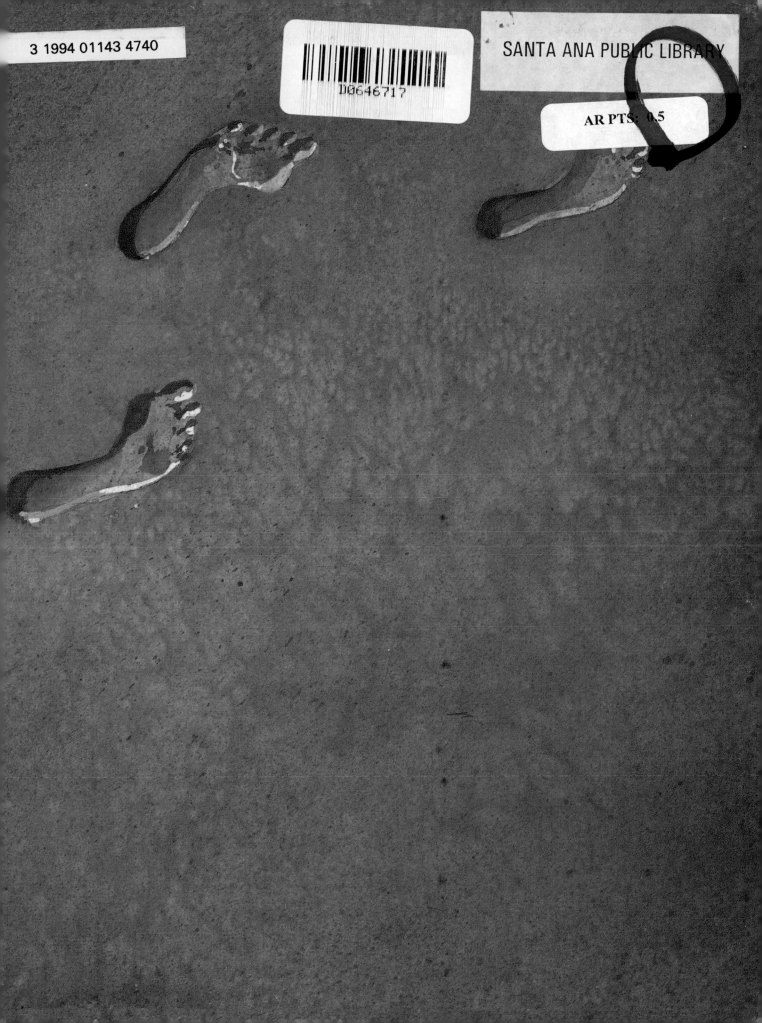

For Sophy

First published in Great Britain in 2001 by
Frances Lincoln Limited, 4 Torriano Mews,
Torriano Avenue, London NW5 2RZ

First American Edition, 2001.
ISBN 0-87358-782-0

Robertson, M. P.
The sandcastle / M.P. Robertson.
p.   cm.
Summary: After a day of watching his strongest sandcastles washed away by a sea that refuses to
obey him, Jack wishes for a real castle in which he is king, and that night his wishes come true.
ISBN 0-87358-782-0 (alk. paper)
[1. Sandcastles—Fiction. 2. Wishes—Fiction. 3. Seashore—Fiction.] I. Title.

PZ7.R54843 San 2001
[E]—dc21   00-045805

345 / 7.5 M / 3-00
Printed in Singapore

The
SANDCASTLE

M. P. Robertson

rising moon

There was nothing in the whole world Jack liked more than building sandcastles. But as strong as he built the walls and as high as he built the towers, he couldn't stop the sea from stealing them away.

At the end of a perfect day, Jack looked proudly at his latest sandcastle.

The tide began to roll in, and Jack stood stubbornly in its path.

"Stay back, sea!" he ordered. "This is my castle. I'm King here."

But the sea just spit at his knees.

Jack looked down and saw a glistening shell at his feet. He placed it on the highest tower of his sandcastle, then shut his eyes tight.

"I wish my sandcastle were as big as a real castle. And I wish that I were King," he said.

When he opened his eyes, he was disappointed to see that his castle hadn't grown an inch and he was still just a boy on a beach.

That evening Jack woke to the squabbling of the gulls. He pulled back the curtains and rubbed his eyes in disbelief. His first wish had come true.

Jack snuck down to the beach, and as he neared the castle, the drawbridge lowered. Jack wasn't scared. This was his castle, so he marched across.

He was met at the gatehouse by a girl whose eyes were as blue as the ocean.

"We've been waiting for you," she said. Then, placing a shell to her lips, she blew a long, salty note.

At her signal the doors to a great hall swung open. Jack was greeted by a fanfare of trumpets and was led through a cheering crowd to a seashell throne. The girl placed a pearly crown on his head.

"Hail, King Jack!" cheered the crowd. "King of the sandcastle!"

His second wish had come true.

A band struck up a tune, and the girl led Jack to the center of the celebration. Into the night they danced. In the merriment, no one heard the waves slapping against the great doors.

Finally, the doors could no longer hold back the sea. With a thunderous crash they gave way. The ocean roared in, sweeping people off their dancing feet.

As the water washed over the crowd, they began to change! Jack watched in amazement as their feet became tails and their skin became scales.

The girl dragged Jack up a staircase to escape the rising tide. From the battlements he watched in horror as the sea bit chunks from his castle.

"Stay back, sea!" he ordered. "I'm a real king now! Look, I've got a crown!"

"You may be a king," said the girl, "but even a king can't stop the sea."

The water continued to rise. Higher and higher they climbed, but the sea was always just one step behind, lapping at their heels.

When Jack reached the top of the tower, he heard the girl say, "Good luck, Jack. Don't forget your fairy tales. You always get three wishes."

Jack looked around, but the girl had vanished. All he saw was the flash of a tail disappearing into the sea.

Still the tide rose. Jack scrambled onto the highest tower. He found the shell that he had placed there the day before. But now it was as big as a boat. He pushed the shell into the water and climbed in.

As the sea swallowed the last of his castle, Jack clung tightly to the shell. "I wish I weren't a king anymore, but just a boy safe at home in bed," he said.

Far in the distance there came a long, salty note. The shell was lifted high on the crest of a wave and swept back to shore.

When Jack woke up, he was no longer on the beach but wrapped warmly in his quilt. Beside him on his pillow lay the shell.

After breakfast he hurried down to the beach. The sea had polished the sand as smooth as a mirror.

As his new sandcastle began to take shape, Jack felt very happy. Being a king was fine, but there was nothing in the whole world Jack liked more than being a boy, on a beach, building sandcastles.

And as the tide turned and licked at the walls of his castle, he just smiled.